Don't Do That!

By Janine Amos and Annabel Spenceley
Consultant Rachael Underwood

CHERRYTREE BOOKS

A CHERRYTREE BOOK

This edition first published in 2007
by Cherrytree Books, part of
The Evans Publishing Group
2A Portman Mansions
Chiltern Street
London
W1U 6NR

Printed in China

British Library Cataloguing in Publication Data.
Amos, Janine
   Don't do that!. - (Good friends)
   1. Friendship - Pictorial works - Juvenile fiction
   2. Children's stories - Pictorial works
   I. Title II. Spenceley, Annabel III. Underwood, Rachael
   823.9'14[J]

ISBN 1842344269
13 digit ISBN 978 1842344262

CREDITS
Editor: Louise John
Designer: D.R.ink
Photography: Gareth Boden
Production: Jenny Mulvanny
Based on the original edition of Don't Do That! published in 1999

With thanks to our models:
The guinea pig
Elizabeth Deller and Ellie Carter
Making a mess
Yolande, Jordan and Brandon Chandler

VISIT OUR WEBSITE
Evans
www.evansbooks.co.uk

The Guinea Pig

Elizabeth shows her friend
Ellie her new guinea pig.
"He's called Gordon,"
says Elizabeth.

"Can I hold him?" asks Ellie. Elizabeth nods.

Elizabeth passes
Gordon to Ellie.

Gordon wriggles.
Ellie squeezes him tight.

"Don't do that!"
shouts Elizabeth.
"You'll hurt him!"

Elizabeth tries to pull Gordon back.
"Let go!" she shouts.

Gordon is frightened.

Ellie lets go of Gordon.

"I only wanted to hold him," says Ellie.

How does Ellie feel?

"Squeezing hurts. You have to hold him gently like this," says Elizabeth.

Ellie strokes Gordon.

Then she holds him gently in her arms.

Making a mess

Jordan is playing in the bathroom. He finds the toilet roll.

He starts to pull.

Jordan pulls it out
of the bathroom.

He makes a pattern all along the hallway.

In the living room,
he wraps toilet roll
around the table.

Brandon sees
Jordan and all
the mess.

"Don't do that!"
shouts Brandon.

Jordan starts to cry loudly.

Mum rushes in. "Look what he's done!" says Brandon.

Mum looks.
She takes a
deep breath.

"Jordan doesn't understand what he's done wrong," says Mum.

Brandon thinks. "Maybe I can show him how to tidy up the mess?" he says.

"Come on, Jordan," says Brandon. "Let's roll this up again so that it can be used."

Jordan smiles.
Tidying up can
be fun too!

TEACHER'S NOTES

By reading these books with young children and inviting them to answer the questions posed in the text, the children can actively work towards aspects of the PSHE and Citizenship curriculum.

Develop confidence and responsibility and making the most of their abilities by
• recognising what they like and dislike, what is fair and unfair and what is right and wrong
• to share their opinions on things that matter to them and explain their views
• to recognise, name and deal with their feelings in a positive way

Develop good relationships and respecting the differences between people
• to recognise how their behaviour affects others
• to listen to other people and play and work co-operatively
• to identify and respect the difference and similarities between people

By using some simple follow up and extension activities, children can also work towards

Citizenship KS1
• to recognise choices that they can make and recognise the difference between right and wrong
• to realise that people and living things have needs, and that they have a responsibility to meet them
• that family and friends should care for each other

EXTENSION ACTIVITY
Drama
• Read through the two stories in *Don't Do That!* Ask the children questions about how the characters would have felt on pages 13 and 25 after being shouted at.
• Ask the children to remember and retell the stories out loud. Ask them if they can think of situations where them shouting might upset or hurt someone. If appropriate list some of the ideas on a whiteboard.
• Put the children into groups of 3 ensuring a good mixture of confidence and group work skill. Ask the children to make up a small 'play' about someone who doesn't explain themselves properly and shouts instead. You may wish to set some boundaries such as no touching or nasty words.
• Give them 3-5 minutes to devise and practise their play. When they have acted out their play, ask them to act it out again but change the ending by having the character not shout. Give 2-3 minutes more for practise.
• Invite volunteers to show the two versions of their play. After the presentations, sit the children in a circle and talk about why people might react to a situation and shout. Discuss how it is better to be calm and think about what you could say that wouldn't upset someone you care about.

These activities can be repeated on subsequent days using the other story in the book or with other stories in the series.